"I'll be you, and you'll be ..."

"Get away from my door," JoJo yelled. "And stop breathing so loud."

"I'm not breathing loud," Winnie yelled back from the other side of the door. "I just want you to play with me."

"I'm busy," JoJo told her. "Go away!"

"You always say you're busy," Winnie said.

"Just go away and stop talking. You're always talking. I can never get any peace around here," JoJo complained.

"I'll stop talking if you play with me." Winnie jiggled the doorknob.

There was a long pause. Then JoJo opened the door. "Okay," she said. "But this time, let's do something different."

"Like what?"

"Like I'll be you, and you'll be me."

OTHER PUFFIN BOOKS YOU MAY ENJOY:

The Bears' House   Marilyn Sachs

Cam Jansen and the Chocolate Fudge Mystery   Adler/Natti

Cam Jansen and the Scary Snake Mystery   Adler/Natti

Elisa in the Middle   Hurwitz/Hoban

The Five Sisters   Mahy/MacCarthy

The Gadget War   Duffey/Wilson

Hannah of Fairfield   Jean Van Leeuwen

Hannah's Helping Hands   Jean Van Leeuwen

Peter and Veronica   Marilyn Sachs

Song Lee and the Hamster Hunt   Kline/Remkiewicz

Third Grade Is Terrible   Baker/Shepherd

Veronica Ganz   Marilyn Sachs

JoJo & Winnie
Sister Stories

Marilyn Sachs
illustrated by **Meredith Johnson**

PUFFIN BOOKS

PUFFIN BOOKS
Published by the Penguin Group
Penguin Putnam Books for Young Readers,
345 Hudson Street, New York, New York 10014, U.S.A.
Penguin Books Ltd, 27 Wrights Lane, London W8 5TZ, England
Penguin Books Australia Ltd, Ringwood, Victoria, Australia
Penguin Books Canada Ltd, 10 Alcorn Avenue, Toronto, Ontario, Canada M4V 3B2
Penguin Books (N.Z.) Ltd, 182-190 Wairau Road, Auckland 10, New Zealand

Penguin Books Ltd, Registered Offices: Harmondsworth, Middlesex, England

First published in the United States of America by Dutton Children's Books,
a division of Penguin Putnam Books for Young Readers, 1999
Published by Puffin Books,
a division of Penguin Putnam Books for Young Readers, 2001

1 3 5 7 9 10 8 6 4 2

THE LIBRARY OF CONGRESS HAS CATALOGED THE DUTTON EDITION AS FOLLOWS:
Sachs, Marilyn. JoJo & Winnie: sister stories / by Marilyn Sachs;
illustrated by Meredith Johnson.—1st ed.
p. cm.
Summary: JoJo suffers the trials of having a younger sister, the irrepressible Winnie.
ISBN 0-525-46005-5 (hc)
[1. Sisters—Fiction.] I. Johnson, Meredith. II. Title. III. Title: JoJo and Winnie.
PZ7.S1187Jo 1999 [Fic]—dc21 98-54734 CIP AC

Puffin Books ISBN 0-14-131113-4

Printed in the United States of America

RL: 2.3

Thank you, Miranda,
thank you, Lena,
for helping me write this book
—M.S.

To Avery
—M.J.

Contents

1 • How JoJo and Winnie
Got Their Names   3

2 • The Easter Egg Hunt   11

3 • Copycats   19

4 • Father's Day   28

5 • Listening Skills   37

6 • "I'll Be You and You'll Be Me"   45

7 • Photobug   55

8 • The Birthday Party   64

JoJo & Winnie
Sister Stories

Chapter 1

How JoJo and Winnie
Got Their Names

When Josephine was nearly four, her parents told her that she was going to be a big sister.

"I want a little sister," she told them. "I have a good name for her."

"It might be a little brother," her father said. "Try to keep an open mind."

"It will be a sister," Josephine said again. "And I will name her Winnie after Winnie-the-Pooh."

"Winnie is not a real name," her father pointed out. "It's only a nickname."

"I like it," Josephine insisted. "I wish I had a nickname."

"Winnie," said her mother softly. "That's not a bad name. If it's a boy, we could name him Winston. And if it's a girl, she could be Winifred."

Before the baby was born, Josephine helped get the room ready. She put the pink bear with the torn nose in the baby's crib. She hung her white party dress with the big pink flowers in the baby's closet. The dress didn't fit her anymore, but it would fit a baby sister. She made a big pink painting to hang up on her sister's wall.

She decided that her sister would have brown eyes and brown hair and look just like she did. Her sister would be quiet and respectful. She would always do what Josephine told her.

It was a sister, all right. And they did name her Winifred. Winifred was tiny. Mostly she lay in her crib, yelling very loud, especially at night. She was nothing like what Josephine had expected.

Mom and Daddy let Josephine hold the baby. When they gave Winifred a bath, Josephine had a new doll to put into the water, too.

Friends and relatives brought presents for Winifred. Most of them also brought presents for Josephine. They took quick looks at the baby. But then they stayed to watch Josephine do her "Ten Little Monkeys" dance and sing "I'm a Little Teapot."

Everybody said how lucky Winifred was to have Josephine for a big sister.

Winifred grew. First she smiled, and then she laughed. Mom and Daddy were impressed. *Big deal!* thought Josephine.

Winifred grew some more. She sat up in her high chair and ate mushy cereal and yucky mashed vegetables. Sometimes, she spit her food all over the table and the floor. Mom and Daddy were still impressed. *Big deal!* thought Josephine.

Winifred began to crawl. "Very early," Mom and Daddy said. *Big deal!* thought Josephine.

Then Winifred crawled into Josephine's room and pulled the head off her fancy Spanish doll. Then she ate two pieces of Josephine's Mickey Mouse puzzle.

Josephine ran away whenever Winifred

followed her. At mealtimes, Winifred always wanted to sit next to Josephine. She put her sticky hands into Josephine's plate. She screamed very loud when Josephine pushed her away.

"I liked it better when we were only three," she told her mother and father. "Four is too many."

"Be patient," her father said. "Soon she will be old enough to be a real playmate for you."

"I don't think so," Josephine said.

Winifred grew and grew. She made a lot of noise. She pulled out all the pots and pans in the kitchen. She knocked over the plants in the living room. She screamed and yelled if anybody tried to stop her. But she didn't say any words. Even when she was nearly a year and a half old, she still did not say any words. Mom and Daddy worried. They read books to her. They repeated words over and over again.

"I said full sentences when I was only one," Josephine reminded them.

Every morning at the breakfast table, Mom repeated words.

"Say *Ma-ma*," Mom said.

Winifred put her hand into Josephine's cereal bowl and pulled out a few Cheerios.

"Say *Da-da*," Daddy said.

"Go away, you pest," Josephine said. She picked up her bowl. Then she moved to a safer seat across the table.

Winifred screamed something.

"Did you hear that?" Mom asked.

"Yes!" Daddy answered. "Isn't it wonderful!"

"What's so wonderful?" Josephine asked.

Winifred screamed again. "JoJo!" she screamed. "JoJo!"

"Her first word," Mom said proudly. "And it's so clear."

"You should feel honored," Daddy said to Josephine. "Your sister's first word is your name. And now you have a good nickname."

"JoJo," Josephine repeated. "I think it's a silly nickname."

But really, she liked it. And she also liked the nickname she had picked for Winifred. "Stop screaming, Winnie," she said to her sister.

Chapter 2

The Easter Egg Hunt

Every year, JoJo's friend Samantha had an Easter egg hunt at her house. JoJo loved going. The year Winnie turned three, she was invited, too.

"You'll have a great time," JoJo told her. "Before we go, we each have to dye twelve hard-boiled eggs. We carry them in a pretty basket to the party. Then we hide each egg in a different part of Samantha's garden. Then everybody hunts for the eggs. You get to keep the ones you find. After the hunt, we all eat cake and ice cream."

"And I will have the most beautiful eggs of all," Winnie said.

JoJo showed Winnie how to dye the eggs by dipping them into colored dyes. Then she showed her how to paste shiny shapes on the eggs. And finally, she showed Winnie how to draw designs on them with markers. JoJo's eggs were all different. She had a blue egg with red dots, a red egg with green stripes, a pink egg with yellow flowers, and an orange egg with wiggly purple lines.

Winnie's eggs were all the same color—a muddy yellow purple, because she insisted on dipping each of them into yellow, red, and blue dye.

"My eggs are very beautiful," Winnie kept saying.

Some of JoJo's other friends brought their little sisters to the Easter egg hunt, too. A few of the little sisters were even younger than Winnie.

Samantha's mother led all the kids into the garden. The other mothers stayed inside.

"Now hide your eggs. Try not to peek at anyone else," Samantha's mother said.

JoJo quickly hid hers in many different places. She tried not to peek, but she did notice that Winnie had hidden all of her ugly, muddy yellow-purple eggs behind the sandbox at the back of the garden. *How silly!* she thought. *Why can't she do anything right?*

"Is everybody ready?" asked Samantha's mother. "When I say THREE, you can start hunting for eggs."

JoJo could hardly wait.

"One . . . two . . . THREE!"

JoJo rushed over to the lilac bush. Samantha always hid at least one of her eggs there. Sure enough, there was a bright yellow egg with bands of blue. JoJo put it into her basket. She hurried over to the slide behind the sandbox. She did not stop to pick up any of Winnie's ugly eggs. She was just reaching out for a bright pink egg under the slide when she heard it.

Everybody heard it. A loud, horrible scream. JoJo knew that scream. But she tried to pretend she did not.

It was Winnie. She was on the ground near the sandbox. She was kicking her legs and screaming. None of the other little sisters were behaving like that. JoJo tried to hide. She crept behind a big snowball bush.

Samantha's mother hurried over to Winnie.

"What's the matter, dear?" she asked. "Are you okay?"

"They took my eggs," Winnie howled. "They took all my eggs!"

Samantha's mother patted Winnie's head. "Well, dear, that's the way it's supposed to be. We don't find our own eggs. We find other people's eggs." She took Winnie's hand. "You come with me, dear. I'll help you find some beautiful eggs. I think I know where a very special egg is hiding."

Winnie didn't stop yelling. Samantha's mother led her over to the pink rosebush near the fence. Winnie continued to yell. Samantha's mother bent down, reached behind the bush, and picked up an egg.

JoJo peeked out from behind the snowball bush.

It was a beautiful egg. It was the most beautiful egg JoJo had ever seen. It was blue on the top and red on the bottom. In between, it sparkled with many different colors.

Samantha's mother held out the beautiful egg to Winnie.

"Here you are, dear," said Samantha's mother. "You can put this egg into your basket."

But Winnie did not put the beautiful egg into her basket. She grabbed it, threw it on the ground, and stamped all over it. The egg broke into tiny, yucky pieces under her shoes.

"I want my own eggs!" she screamed. "I want all of them!"

JoJo ducked behind the snowball bush again.

Winnie kept screaming, so everybody gave the ugly eggs back to her. Mom decided that Winnie had better leave early. Before the cake and ice cream.

But Winnie didn't mind skipping the cake and ice cream. She was happy because she was leaving just the way she had come—with all her muddy yellow-purple eggs back in her own basket.

JoJo was happy, too. After Winnie left, she came out from behind the snowball bush. She had found five eggs while she was hiding there. She ended up finding more eggs than anybody else. And she sat next to Samantha while they ate their cake and ice cream. Best of all, nobody thought it was *her* fault that she had such a bratty little sister.

Chapter 3

Copycats

"Cousin Mollie is sick," Mom said to the girls. It was a rainy day in September. "She'll have to stay home at least a week. I think it might cheer her up if you made her get-well cards."

"I don't want to," Winnie said. (Winnie said "I don't want to" a lot of the time.)

"Well, I do," JoJo said. Mom smiled at JoJo and tried to ignore Winnie.

JoJo knew she was a very fine artist. Everybody said so. Her pictures were hanging up in every room in the house. Winnie mostly made squiggles. There were only a few of her pictures hanging up.

JoJo got her box of markers. She settled down at the kitchen table. Then she laid a large, pale yellow piece of construction paper on the table in front of her. After that, she picked up a red marker. Then she put it down and picked up a purple marker.

Winnie watched over her shoulder.

"Stop breathing on my neck," JoJo said.

"I'm not breathing on your neck," Winnie replied. "I'm just breathing."

"Mom, make her stop," JoJo cried. "She's bothering me, and I can't think."

Winnie burst into tears. "I'm not bothering you! I want to make a picture, too."

"Well, go get your own markers and sit over there at the other end of the table," JoJo told her. "And don't copy me."

JoJo put down the purple marker and picked up an orange one.

Winnie sat down in the seat across the table. She rattled her markers, and she watched JoJo.

Suddenly JoJo knew exactly what she wanted to draw. She put down the orange marker and picked up a pink one and a green one. On the pale yellow paper, she drew three huge pink flowers. They had green leaves and graceful stems. JoJo thought it was the most beautiful drawing she had ever made in her whole life.

"That's a lovely card, JoJo," her mother said. "Now all you have to do is sign your name and fold it. I'll find an envelope for it."

JoJo looked at the three beautiful pink flowers. She took a deep breath.

"I'm going to keep this," she said to her mother. "I'll make another one for Mollie."

"Look at mine, Mom! Look at mine!" Winnie cried. She held up her drawing. It was a flower with a long, thin, squiggly green stem that filled up most of the paper. There was only a little room left at the top for some sloppy pink petals.

"That's good, Winnie," Mom said. "That's a real flower you made. You've never made a flower before. I'll help you sign your name, and we'll send it to Mollie."

"No," Winnie said. "I'm going to make her another one, just like JoJo."

JoJo thought Winnie's drawing was ugly. As usual, she was trying to copy JoJo. Then JoJo picked up a purple marker and a yellow one. She folded a green piece of paper in half and began to draw. Today was a rainy day, so she drew four children wearing yellow raincoats. They carried purple umbrellas.

JoJo looked at the finished drawing. It was just as good as her first one.

"That's very pretty, too," said Mom. "I'm sure Cousin Mollie will like it."

JoJo took a deep breath. "No," she told her mother. "I want to keep this one, too."

"Look at mine, look at mine," said Winnie. She held up a piece of paper with red squiggles holding on to purple squiggles.

"It's very colorful," Mom said. "I'll help you sign it, and you can put the stamp on the envelope."

"No," said Winnie. "I want to keep this one, too. Just like JoJo."

"Now, girls," Mom said in her unfriendly voice, "you are both acting very selfish."

"But it's hard to give my pictures away

when they're so beautiful. Every picture I make is something special," said JoJo.

"Me, too," Winnie echoed.

"Stop being such a copycat," said JoJo.

Winnie picked up a marker. "I'm not a copycat," she said. She started drawing.

"You're setting a very bad example for your sister," Mom told JoJo. "It's wonderful to share something good with another person and make her happy—especially your favorite cousin, Mollie. And besides, you can always draw something else for yourself."

JoJo grabbed a black crayon and a piece of brown paper. She folded it carelessly and quickly scribbled all over it. The picture was so ugly, she did not want to keep it. She signed her name messily and handed it to Mom.

Mom shook her head, but before she could

say anything, Winnie yelled, "I'm finished! I'm finished!" She held up her picture.

JoJo looked at it. She was surprised. Winnie had made a drawing of three faces that looked like faces. There was a big face. "That's Mollie," Winnie explained. There was a middle-sized face. "That's JoJo," she continued. And there was a little face. "That's me," Winnie said. Each face had eyes, a nose, and a smiling mouth.

"Why, Winnie," said Mom, "this is a very pretty picture. I guess you're going to be a good artist, too, just like JoJo."

"Yes," said Winnie, "I am a good artist, but I am *not* like JoJo."

"How come?" JoJo demanded.

"Because I want to send my picture to Cousin Mollie. *I* don't want to be selfish."

JoJo grabbed a fresh piece of paper. She

used all of her markers. When she finished, there were three girls in pretty dresses, each smiling and waving. It was the most beautiful picture she had made that day.

"Here," she said to Mom. "You can send this to Mollie. I'm not selfish, either."

"Copycat," said Winnie.

Chapter 4

Father's Day

"Today is Father's Day," JoJo told Winnie early one Sunday morning.

"I know," Winnie said. "I planted a flower for him in one of my old pink sneakers."

"Yes, yes!" JoJo waved her off. "And I made him a picture frame with a school photo of me inside. But I think we should bring him breakfast in bed today. Let's go down to the kitchen and decide what to make."

"How about pancakes and sausages?" Winnie suggested as they hurried downstairs.

"We're not allowed to cook anything, remember? We'll have to make him something cold." JoJo opened the refrigerator.

"I can put my Froot Loops in a bowl," Winnie offered. "Maybe the beautiful cherry bowl."

"He doesn't like Froot Loops," JoJo said patiently.

"Well, how about a peanut butter sandwich? That's cold."

"Good idea," said JoJo. "He likes peanut butter sandwiches. Especially on cinnamon raisin bread." She stood on a chair and looked into the freezer. "Here's a loaf. I'll just take out two pieces."

"Give them to me," cried Winnie. "I'll toast them."

"Now, Winnie," JoJo said, "you know you're not allowed to use the toaster. But I can."

JoJo put two pieces of cinnamon raisin bread into the toaster. She took the jar of peanut butter out of the refrigerator.

"I'll make the sandwich," Winnie said.

"You make sloppy sandwiches and get the peanut butter all over your fingers," JoJo told her. "I'll make the sandwich."

She took the cinnamon raisin bread out of the toaster. Then she put it onto the Seattle Mariners baseball plate. The whole family rooted for the Seattle Mariners. Everybody fought over that plate. Since today was Father's Day, it was only fair that Daddy should have it. JoJo opened the jar of peanut butter.

"I want to do something, too!" Winnie shouted.

"Shh! You'll wake Daddy." JoJo spread peanut butter very neatly on one piece of the toast. Then she carefully fitted the other piece exactly on top. She chose the round, shiny black tray. She put the Mariners plate right in the middle of it. Carefully, she poured some apple juice into a pretty blue glass.

"What can *I* do?" Winnie shouted.

"Shh! Why don't you go outside and pick a few flowers to put on the tray? You can do that without messing up."

"I don't want to pick flowers," Winnie cried. "I want to make something for Daddy." She opened the refrigerator and looked inside.

JoJo put a pretty red napkin and a banana onto the tray. Winnie was still frowning and looking into the refrigerator. Then JoJo went out into the garden herself. She picked a yellow daisy and a white one.

When she returned, Winnie was grinning.

"Why are you grinning?" JoJo asked.

"Because I'm happy," Winnie told her. "Let's take the breakfast to Daddy."

JoJo put the daisies on the tray and straightened out the sandwich.

"Come on, let's go," Winnie urged.

JoJo carried the tray up the stairs. They met Mom on her way down. "We're taking Daddy breakfast in bed for Father's Day," Winnie told her.

"Oh!" said Mom. "But I was going to make him pancakes and sausages."

"You can make some for us," Winnie said. "We made a special, delicious sandwich for Daddy."

Mom followed them into the bedroom. Daddy was still sleeping. Both girls shouted, "HAPPY FATHER'S DAY!"

"*Wmpf!*" said Daddy, opening one eye.

"We're bringing you breakfast in bed," Winnie said. "Hurry up! Go to the bathroom, wash up, and come right back!"

Daddy did what he was told. When he returned, both of his eyes were open, and he was smiling. He slipped back into bed. JoJo placed the tray in his lap.

"Yummy! Yummy!" Daddy said. He picked up the apple juice and sipped it. "Very refreshing," he said. "And look at this beautiful sandwich." He took a little bite out of it. "What is it?"

"It's a peanut butter sandwich," JoJo explained. "I made it myself."

"I put some salami in it," Winnie con-

tinued. "It's a peanut butter and salami sandwich. So we both made it."

"Oh!" said Daddy, putting the sandwich back on the plate.

"You spoil everything!" JoJo shouted at Winnie.

"Well, I wanted to make something for Daddy, too, and you wouldn't let me!" Winnie shouted back.

"I think I'll go downstairs and make some pancakes and sausages," Mom said.

Daddy picked up the sandwich and looked at it. He took a teeny, tiny bite. The girls watched him slowly chewing and waited.

"This is certainly interesting." Daddy swallowed. He took a bigger bite, chewed it faster, and swallowed. "You know—I think— I think—this is really very good." Daddy finished the whole sandwich, then the banana and the apple juice.

Later, when he joined them in the kitchen, he said he didn't want any pancakes and sausages. Instead, he made himself another peanut butter and salami sandwich on cinnamon raisin bread. "This is the best Father's Day ever," he told JoJo and Winnie.

Chapter 5

Listening Skills

Winnie liked to talk. All the time. Daddy said she was making up for the first year and a half of her life. Back then she did not talk at all.

Now that she was five, she liked to talk to her friends in her kindergarten class. She liked to talk during snack time and during recess. She also liked to talk whenever other people were talking, including her teacher, Ms. Chu.

"We are going to have to work on your listening skills," Ms. Chu said to Winnie one day.

"I don't like listening," Winnie told Ms. Chu.

"That may be so," said Ms. Chu. "But it would be a very noisy world if nobody listened."

"It's not interesting to listen," said Winnie.

"Maybe you would be surprised if you tried it. I want you to sit quietly at your table. Keep listening until you hear something interesting. Then, just raise your hand, and I will call on you."

Winnie flopped into her chair, made a mean face, and rattled her lunch box noisily.

Ms. Chu told her to stop. Finally, Winnie began to listen.

She heard Dylan cough.

She heard Rosie laugh.

She heard Carter and William knock down a crooked tower of blocks.

Winnie raised her hand.

"Yes, Winnie," said Ms. Chu. "What did you hear that was interesting?"

"Nothing," said Winnie. "Now can I talk?"

"No," said Ms. Chu. "I'm sure if you listen you'll hear something interesting."

"What if I don't?" Winnie demanded.

"Just stop talking," said Ms. Chu. "And start listening. Right now!"

Again, Winnie listened.

She heard Ms. Chu tell Marie to pick up her jacket from the floor.

She heard Robert blow his nose.

She heard the window shade rattling against the window.

Winnie raised her hand.

"Yes, Winnie," said Ms. Chu. "Did you hear anything interesting this time?"

"I heard the window shade rattling against the window," Winnie said.

"Did you think that was interesting?" inquired Ms. Chu.

"Not really," said Winnie.

"I think you'd better keep listening," said Ms. Chu.

This time, Winnie wrinkled up her face, cocked her head to one side, and listened.

She heard Ms. Chu tell the class that they were all going on a field trip to the zoo in a couple of weeks. That was interesting. But before she could raise her hand, she heard something else. She heard Rebecca tell Tina that since Clara had moved away, she could be her best friend. That was interesting, too. But suddenly, she heard Sam knock over the easel where Henrietta was painting. And she heard Henrietta yell as the paint spilled over her shoes. That was very interesting. Her hand was halfway up when she heard something else. Something very soft and very, very interesting. She raised her hand.

But Ms. Chu was busy cleaning up Henrietta's shoes and yelling at Sam. Winnie waved her hand. Finally, she stood up.

"Oh, yes, Winnie. I'm sure you've heard some interesting things just now."

"I sure did," said Winnie.

"I suppose you heard me tell the children that all of us were going on a field trip."

"Yes, that was interesting. And I heard

Rebecca tell Tina she could be her best friend. And I heard when Sam knocked over the easel, too. But I heard something else that's even more interesting."

"And what could that be?" asked Ms. Chu, wiping up a big blob of blue paint from the floor.

"I need to find out," said Winnie, jumping up. She could still hear it. Somebody was humming. She followed the hum until it grew louder and louder. Finally, she stood looking down at Jesse. He was turning the pages of a book and humming.

"I know that song," Winnie told Jesse. "It's my favorite song, and I know all the words."

"It's my favorite song, too," Jesse said, looking up and smiling at her.

"I didn't know that," Winnie said, smiling back.

Later, Ms. Chu let Winnie and Jesse sing "London Bridge Is Falling Down" to the whole class. Many of the other children joined in, too. But Winnie was the only one who knew all the words.

Chapter 6

"I'll Be You and You'll Be Me"

"Get away from my door," JoJo yelled. "And stop breathing so loud."

"I'm not breathing loud," Winnie yelled back from the other side of the door. "I just want you to play with me."

"I'm busy," JoJo told her. "Go away!"

"You *always* say you're busy," Winnie said. "What are you so busy doing?"

"I'm reading."

"You're always reading."

JoJo did not answer.

"Please!" Winnie said.

JoJo did not answer.

"We can take all our dolls to the doctor. You can be the doctor."

No answer.

"You can even give them shots."

"Just go away and stop talking. You're always talking. I can never get any peace around here," JoJo complained.

"I'll stop talking if you play with me." Winnie jiggled the doorknob.

"Go away!"

"I know," Winnie said finally. "Let's dress up."

There was a long pause. Then JoJo opened the door. "Okay," she said. "But this time, let's do something different."

"Like what?"

"Like I'll be you, and you'll be me."

"How do we do that?" Winnie asked.

"I'll dress up in your clothes. You'll dress up in mine. Then we'll act like each other."

JoJo went into Winnie's room. She pulled on Winnie's pink-and-purple fish T-shirt and her purple leggings. The T-shirt came to just above JoJo's belly button. The leggings reached just below her knees. She couldn't fit her feet into Winnie's shoes, so she went barefoot.

Winnie slipped her feet into JoJo's shoes. They were too big and made clunky noises when she walked. JoJo's red, white, and black zebra T-shirt came down to her knees. She had to roll up JoJo's jeans because they dragged on the floor.

Then they were ready to be each other.

"I want to play in your room," JoJo

whined, trying to sound like Winnie. "I want to play with your ballerina puzzle. I want to play with your Barbie doll. You never let me play with your Barbie doll. I'm going to tell Mom. I'm going to tell Daddy."

"You stay out of my room," Winnie snarled, trying to sound like JoJo. "You're a spoiled brat, and I hate you."

She went into JoJo's room and slammed the door.

"I hate you, too!" JoJo shouted outside the door to her room. "You're the meanest kid in Seattle. You're the meanest kid in the world."

"Get lost!" Winnie yelled from behind the door.

JoJo went into Winnie's room and slammed the door behind her. She took all Winnie's books off the bookshelves and scattered them around on the floor. She threw Winnie's pillow on the floor and her dolls, too. She tossed out all the socks from Winnie's sock drawer. Then she pulled all the pieces out of Winnie's jungle puzzle and put them into the drawer. It was a lot of fun. Winnie always scattered things around in JoJo's room. *I wonder what she's doing now?* JoJo thought.

JoJo left Winnie's room and stood outside her own door. It was very, very quiet in there. "Don't you dare mess up my room," she called nervously.

"I'm not messing up your room, Winnie," Winnie said from behind the door. "I'm messing up *my* room."

JoJo rattled the doorknob. She yelled, "You'd better let me in right now!"

"Go play in your own room," Winnie

yelled back. "I want my privacy."

JoJo kicked the door and yelled so loud that Mom came running up the stairs. "What's going on?" Mom demanded. "Stop kicking your door! And why are you wearing Winnie's clothes?"

"She won't let me into my room," JoJo yelled. "I want her to open the door, and she won't."

"Winnie," Mom yelled. "Open this door right now!"

Winnie opened the door. "I'm not Winnie," she said. "I'm JoJo, and she's Winnie."

"I'm not playing anymore," JoJo said. "It's a stupid game, and it's no fun being you."

She shoved Winnie out of the way and hurried into her room. Nothing was messed up. There was an open book on JoJo's bed.

"I was reading," Winnie explained. "Just the way you always do when I want to play with you."

"I don't always read," JoJo said. "Sometimes I play with you. And besides, you don't know how to read."

"Your dolls are too stuck-up. I like mine better anyway," Winnie said. She walked into her own room and let out a yell. "Mom! Just look how she messed up my room. Make her clean it up!"

"I didn't mess up *your* room," JoJo explained. "When I messed it up, I was you. Now I'm me, and you're you. So you have to clean it up."

"JoJo!" Mom said. "You clean up that room right now!"

JoJo grumbled, but she put all the books back on the shelves. She picked up the pillow and the dolls. She fitted all the pieces together in the puzzle. It took some time, but finally everything was back in its right place. Then she pulled off Winnie's clothes. Winnie pulled off JoJo's. Each of them got dressed in her own clothes again.

"What can we play now?" Winnie asked.

"Nothing," JoJo told her. She went into her own room and closed the door.

Outside, Winnie whined, "Let me in, JoJo."

"Get lost!" JoJo yelled.

"I'll tell Mom," Winnie cried. "I'll tell Daddy."

JoJo looked around her room. Everything was in its right place except for the open book on her bed. She picked it up. It was *Little House in the Big Woods,* one of her favorites. She hadn't read it in a long time.

Outside the door, Winnie rattled the doorknob.

"Go away," JoJo said, but not in a very mean voice. "I want my privacy."

She settled herself on the bed and began to read. She was glad she was herself again.

Chapter 7

Photobug

"There are too many pictures of Winnie in the family album," JoJo told her father one day. "There are not enough of me."

"How can that be?" Daddy asked, surprised. "Since you were born first, there are certainly more pictures of you than of Winnie."

He picked up the album and began flipping through it.

"Just look!" he said to JoJo. "Here's a picture of you when you were first born. And here's one of you on your way home from the hospital. And just look at this one. Don't you look cute in your fancy red-and-white sweater and cap that Grandma knit for you?"

JoJo quickly turned the pages. "But look here, Daddy. Once Winnie was born, you took lots of pictures of her."

"Well, yes, we did. But there are also lots of you. And there are even more of the two of you together."

"No, no, no!" JoJo grumbled. "There are too many of her. I wish I had an album just for me. I wish I had my own camera, too."

"Hmm," Daddy said.

For Christmas, JoJo received a camera and a photo album. It even had her name

—JOSEPHINE—printed in gold on the cover.

JoJo loved to take pictures. She took pictures of her friends Samantha and Alison skating. She took pictures of her parents at the school picnic. She took pictures of Grandma and Grandpa on their porch. And she took pictures of Cousin Jeffrey wearing his Seattle Mariners cap.

Most of her pictures turned out sharp and clear.

"You certainly do take good pictures," Mom said. "I think you have a real talent."

JoJo arranged her pictures very carefully inside her album. Since she had taken all of the pictures, there weren't any of her. She asked Dad to snap one. She put the picture on the first page of her album. Underneath it, she wrote her name with a gold marker.

She labeled each of her other pictures the same way.

"But there aren't any of me," Winnie complained.

"There are plenty of you in the family album," JoJo told her.

Winnie complained to Mom, and she complained to Daddy.

"You're being very mean," Daddy told JoJo. "You're making Winnie feel terrible."

So at Winnie's sixth birthday party, JoJo took the pictures.

"Just look at those candles on the cake!" Mom said. "It's wonderful how you caught them shining so brightly."

"But you can't see me," Winnie complained. "My face is hidden behind the cake."

"And just look how you caught Winnie

swinging at the piñata! I love the way her dress is swirling around her legs."

"But it's the *back* of me," Winnie pointed out. "You can see the back of my dress, but you can't see the front of me."

JoJo had taken many pictures of the other children at the party. Everyone thought the pictures were great. Some parents wanted more than one copy.

"But there isn't one good picture of me," Winnie said. "She always leaves me out."

Grandma and Grandpa bought a subscription for JoJo to a magazine called *Photobugs*. All of the photographs in the magazine were taken by kids. The magazine had many good tips on how to take original, artistic photos.

JoJo began trying to take more original, artistic pictures. She went to the zoo and

snapped the flamingos with their pink feathers and black beaks. She snapped a plum tree in bloom with snowy white flowers. She caught a cloudy sky outside her bedroom window.

When the magazine announced a contest, JoJo decided to enter it. The first prize was $200. The second prize was $100. And the third prize was twelve rolls of film.

JoJo took pictures at the park. She took pictures at Green Lake. She took pictures anywhere she saw something she liked. She kept trying to remember all the tips she had read in the magazine.

One day she was at Green Lake with Mom and Winnie. She had one last shot left on her roll of film. She was saving it for a very special picture. Suddenly, she saw exactly what she needed. There was a white heron, standing on one leg on a rock in the lake. The wind was rippling its feathers. It was close to dusk, and the heron looked very white against the darkening sky.

JoJo moved closer to the heron. She tried to be very careful not to startle it. The heron stood there, as still as a statue. JoJo's finger moved slowly down on the shutter button. Now! But just as she clicked, there was a sudden flurry of movement. The heron flew away, and there stood Winnie grinning at her.

JoJo wanted to push Winnie into the lake. "You ruined it!" JoJo wailed. "The best picture I ever took. You ruin everything!"

When the roll of film was developed, many of the pictures were beautiful. The one of Pike Place Market with its brilliant colors was a favorite of Dad's. Mom liked the one of Alison holding a huge bunch of yellow daffodils. And there was one of a rowboat against a red sky at sunset. Grandpa said he would frame it and hang it up in his house.

But everyone agreed that one picture was far better than all the others. It showed a white heron with its feathers rippling. It also showed a young girl. The girl's hair rippled as she laughed and reached out toward the startled bird. Everything in that picture was original and artistic.

JoJo's picture did not win first prize. A twelve-year-old won first prize. And an eleven-year-old won second prize. But JoJo won third prize.

Her picture, along with the pictures of the other winners, was published in *Photobugs*. All over the country her picture of the heron and Winnie was seen by many, many people.

JoJo even put the picture into her album.

Chapter 8

The Birthday Party

Winnie watched as each child arrived at the
birthday party.

Rosie wore a pink frilly dress. She carried
a small present wrapped in gold paper with a
gold bow.

Judy wore a blue-and-red-striped dress.
She carried a large square present wrapped
in bright yellow paper with a bunch of red
squiggles on top.

Marie was also carrying a large square present. But her wrapping was green with a white bow. Winnie wondered if it was the same present as Judy's.

A car pulled up, and just as Melanie got out, JoJo came into the living room. "What did you do with my ballerina puzzle?" she asked in an angry voice. "Two pieces are missing."

Winnie did not turn from the window or answer.

"I keep telling you to keep your hands off my things," JoJo shouted. "And stay out of my room. Do you hear me?"

Winnie did not reply. Two girls she didn't know were now going up the front steps.

JoJo stamped behind Winnie. Winnie could hear her breathing, but she didn't turn around. She was busy watching the two girls.

JoJo dropped a hand on Winnie's shoulder.

She started to say, "Did you hear what . . ."
Then she stopped talking. She stood there,
looking out the window. She watched
with Winnie as Ariel opened the door and
smiled at the two girls. Ariel was wearing a
white dress with big red polka dots. Even
from across the street, you could see how
big they were. Ariel smiled and reached
out for the presents. Then the girls went
through the door. JoJo could see the
balloons inside.

"Oh!" said JoJo. "I didn't know today was
Ariel's birthday."

"I did," said Winnie.

"How come she didn't invite you?" JoJo
asked.

"I don't know," Winnie said. "I thought
she was my friend."

"Did you have a fight?"

"No."

"Did you say something mean to her?"

"No."

"Well, who cares about her," JoJo said. "You won't invite her to your birthday party, that's all."

"But I *did* invite her to my birthday party. Don't you remember?"

"Of course I remember. But from now on, you won't."

"She always used to invite me to her birthday parties."

"Maybe she's only asking the kids in her class."

"Judy isn't in her class. She's in mine."

"Well, I never liked Ariel anyway."

"I did." Winnie turned around now, and JoJo saw her sister's eyes fill up with tears.

"Come upstairs with me," JoJo said. "We'll play a game or something."

"I don't want to," Winnie said. "And I

think those missing pieces of the ballerina puzzle are under your bed."

"That's all right," JoJo said. "Don't worry about them. Just come away from the window. I'll let you . . . I'll let you play with my music box."

"I don't want to play with your music box." Winnie turned back and watched as Elena hurried up the stairs. When Ariel opened the door, she could see the kids inside laughing.

"They're having a good time," Winnie said. "And I bet Ariel's mom made those special cupcakes with chocolate sprinkles."

"Hey, Winnie," JoJo said. "Let's have our own party."

"Who will come?" Winnie asked. "All my friends are at Ariel's party."

"We'll invite our dolls and bears. We'll have a bigger party than Ariel's."

Winnie stopped looking out the window. She and JoJo gathered all their dolls and bears together and brought them downstairs. By the time they bunched them around the kitchen table, Winnie was feeling better. Mom made them hot chocolate with tiny marshmallows. She let them eat the frozen brownies she was saving for the school picnic. JoJo took pictures of all of them celebrating.

Later, some of the dolls felt sick because they had eaten too many brownies and marshmallows. Winnie and JoJo put them to bed. Winnie didn't feel so great, either.

"Can I lie down in your bed?" Winnie asked.

JoJo thought for a second. "I guess so," she said finally.

JoJo tucked Winnie into her bed, then read her one story after another.

"You know what?" Winnie said to her.

"What?"

"This is the first time you've been nice to me for a whole afternoon."

"Well," JoJo said. "I don't like it when other people are mean to you."

"Most of the time they're not," Winnie said. "Maybe that's why you are."

"It's hard work being nice to you for so long," JoJo said. "I can't wait for tomorrow."

"I can," Winnie said, nestling down in JoJo's bed. "And now, will you read me another story?"